'WOMEN HEAD TO WORK AT FORD FACTORIES'

The Detroit Press

June 1, 1940
EXTRA

Rosie | *Stronger than Steel*

BY **Lindsay Ward**

ROSIE THE RIVET
DOES IT AL

'ORD SHIPS 10,000 TRACTORS TO ENGLAND'

The Detroit Press

March 11, 1941
EXTRA

WORLD AT WAR

ROOSEVELT SIGNS LEND-LEASE ACT

FORD TO
PRODUCE
10,000
TRACTORS

$\mathcal{R}$efrigerators, fences,
old cars, and a toaster . . .

all melted down
to build me up strong.

Of scrap and sweat I was forged to be tough.
With each weld, each rivet,
and each spark that was shed,

I rose from the ground.
A one-of-a-kind.

Down on the floor, the ladies would sing:

This is our Rosie,
stronger than steel.

She'll plow all the land
with a turn of her wheel.

Harvest the fields.
Take care of your farm.

Do this, dear Rosie,
and keep out of harm.

Then they left their mark.
"To remember us by,"
they whispered in close.

Grateful, I delivered my oath:

I'll plow and I'll dig.
I'll dig and I'll plow.
No matter the job,
this is my vow.

Then we said our goodbyes
through the cracks of my crate.

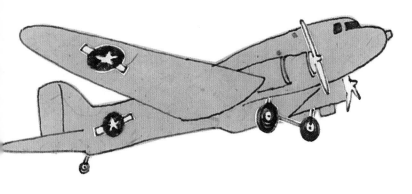

I traveled great distances.

Through air and by sea.

On truck and by train.

In darkness. And silence.

Finally we stopped, and my crate opened up. . . .

Then I saw it . . . all covered in weeds.

My field. My place.

My farm in need.

The tall grass tickled
as my blades dug deep.
I felt the ground churn
as the dirt splashed up.

Amidst the endless green,
covered in mud,
beside the brave Land Girls,
I found my new home.

We worked day and night.

We grew many crops . . .

Wheat and barley. Oats and potatoes.

Sugar beets, currants, apples, tomatoes.

They all rose up to the tune of my song:

I plow and I dig.
I dig and I plow.
No matter the job,
this is my vow.

Some days were endless, heavy with fear, hiding in fields . . .
quietly moving beneath the shadows above.

Whispering over and over . . .

I plow and I dig.
I dig and I plow.
No matter the job,
this is my vow.

BARLEY

But more crops were needed!
Load after load, sent out to the troops.
To feed them. To help them. To win the war!

We milked and sheared.

We picked and packed.

I plow and I dig.
I dig and I plow.
No matter the job,
this is my vow.

The work was tough . . .
but we were tougher.

Clearing and logging.
Hauling and fixing.
Day after day.
Year after year.

Then one spring day . . .
in field after field—cheers rang out!
A celebration spread throughout the world.

The war was over!

Time passed and the world around changed.
New, young tractors took to the fields.
I taught them to plow. To dig and to sow.
To churn up the dirt, and make it all grow.

And then one day . . .
	a bang and a growl.

In a puff of black smoke there I was, stuck.

Hauled into the barn, the farmers all tinkered.

My eyes grew heavy as I drifted to sleep.
And I dreamt of the ladies who built me and sang:

**This is our Rosie,
stronger than steel.**

**She'll plow all the land
with a turn of her wheel.**

It must have been days, I wasn't quite sure.
Then, deep from my engine . . .

A shudder.

A flutter . . .

I sputtered to life!

Real rubber tires! Shiny new paint!
And my rose, a gift all those years ago,
had blossomed, full and bright—

wrapping me in petals.

Rosie

Stronger than Steel

Thank you, dear Rosie,
for all you have done.
Without your service,
we wouldn't have won!

All those years ago, I'd given my oath to the women
who'd built me and farmed alongside me.
Bravely, together we summoned our courage.
Together we worked and fought to be free.

Author's Note

The idea behind this book began to form when I noticed women in my town mowing their lawns with tractors from the 1940s and 1950s. Shortly thereafter, I saw the same vintage tractors immaculately restored at the county fair, and I started to wonder about them. As I began to research, I focused on tractors manufactured during World War II. I learned about the vital role of women in farming in the US and England during the war, crop production in the war effort, the Lend-Lease Act, and more about Rosie the Riveter too.

I read about women who had acted with courage and strength and made important contributions to the success of the war effort. I found that I wanted to tell their story—at least the story of some of them—in a way that children might understand and in a way that stretched beyond our borders to show how the United States joined forces with other countries for the greater good. *Rosie* is not based on a real tractor—it's a work of fiction set against a historical background, meant to honor the work of two important groups of women during World War II: female factory workers in the US and the Women's Land Army in England.

Rosie's story starts in the United States, where she's built by a group of women who represent those who stepped into vital roles in factories, commonly referred to as Rosie the Riveter. While some women had previously held factory jobs, millions more joined the labor force between 1940 and 1945 to help build airplanes, ships, and munitions while the men who would normally have held these jobs were serving in the armed forces. Women also began to hold other jobs that had, in many cases, previously been done only by men. Some 350,000 joined the US armed forces. It was tough work, but it helped turn the tide in the war. For some women—including, as I learned, my husband's great-grandmother, Helen Briggs—it was also exhilarating to be part of the workforce for the first time in their lives and to have responsibilities outside of the domestic sphere.

Women of color played a huge role during this time—often facing challenges while trying to do their part. Some employers didn't want to hire them, and some white women didn't want to work alongside them. In 1941, President Roosevelt issued an executive order preventing discrimination in defense industries and civil service jobs, though that did not keep factories from having segregated facilities or factory workers from having racist attitudes. In some factories, African American workers would not have worked alongside white workers; in others, they would have, as in this story.

In the United Kingdom, the war started in 1939, and the Women's Land Army (WLA), which had previously existed in World War I, was re-formed that June. Women left their homes and headed for rural farms, taking on the tough jobs no one else was around to do, like planting

Women's Land Army members farming in 1943. (AP/Shutterstock)

TIMELINE

June 1939
Women's Land Army re-forms.

September 1939
World War II begins.

1940
American women begin working in factories at a rapid rate.

March 1941
President Franklin D. Roosevelt signs the Lend-Lease Act.

and harvesting fields, logging trees, catching rats, hauling crops, plowing, and driving and fixing tractors. Some women volunteered for this effort—they were commonly referred to as "Land Girls." In 1941, it became mandatory for unmarried women between eighteen and sixty to register for war work. In December of 1941, single women between the ages of twenty and thirty (later expanded to ages nineteen to forty-three) could be conscripted into serving the war effort, including as part of the WLA. By 1944, over seven million women contributed to war work in some capacity in the UK.

Prior to the war, the UK had imported much of its food. During the first part of the war, German U-boats blocked many of these imports, as well as other fuel tankers and cargo ships. It was critical for enough food to be grown to sustain those who stayed at home and those who served. More than 80,000 women worked in the WLA, helping to increase crop production and convert unused pastures. Although food was rationed and some imports did come through, the WLA's work was instrumental in ensuring the British population didn't starve.

The US did not enter the war until December of 1941, but in March of that year, President Roosevelt signed the Lend-Lease Act. This allowed England and other countries to receive much-needed wartime supplies from the United States without having to pay for them until after the end of the war. Supplies included planes, trucks, wartime vehicles, and tractors.

Ford Motor Company sent 10,000 tractors as part of this effort, including Ford-Ferguson N models, which were inexpensive, tough, and could handle almost any job. Rosie is a combination of tractor models manufactured from 1939 to 1942. She's a pared-down wartime model with steel wheels as opposed to rubber, which would have been rationed and used elsewhere during the war. She would have been manufactured in machine gray and painted green once she arrived in

Workers welding at Ford's plant in Willow Run in 1942. (Nara Archives/Shutterstock)

England to blend in with the landscape and be less visible from bomber planes. Since this story doesn't show factory workers in England, I chose to make Rosie green before she left the United States. Her rose decoration wouldn't have been used—it's included here as a tribute to her name and to Rosie the Riveters.

I found a couple of written sources about the WLA using the 10,000 tractors that Ford shipped under the Lend-Lease Act as well as a number of photos of WLA members on those tractors; however, one expert indicated it was unclear if the bulk of those tractors were used by the WLA or if many may have gone elsewhere in the UK. While tractors were shipped from the US to England in 1941, and women worked in US factories then (including Ford factories), I was unable to find definitive documentation indicating that American women built that group of tractors.

I'm incredibly grateful for those women who came before me, paving the way. We wouldn't be where we are today without them. *Rosie* is my thank-you to those women.

—*Lindsay Ward*

1941
Ford ships 10,000 tractors to England.

December 1941
The United States enters WWII after the bombing of Pearl Harbor.

May 1945
Victory is declared in Europe; May 8 is celebrated as V-E Day.

For all the Rosies.
—L.W.

**To learn more about the Women's Land Army, Rosie the Riveter, or Ford tractors,
check out the sources below:**

Colman, Penny. *Rosie the Riveter: Women Working on the Home Front in World War II.* New York, New York: Crown Publishers, Inc., 1995.

Doyle, Jack, "Rosie the Riveter 1941–1945," The Pop History Dig, https://www.pophistorydig.com/topics/rosie-the-riveter-1941-1945/

Gibbard, Stuart. *The Ford Tractor Story: Part One: Dearborn to Dagenham 1917-1964.* England: Japonica Press and Old Pond Publishing, 1998.

Mason, Amanda, "The Workers That Kept Britain Going During the Second World War," Imperial War Museums, February 5, 2018, https://www.iwm.org.uk/history/the-workers-that-kept-britain-going-during-the-second-world-war

Williams, Michael. *Ford & Fordson Tractors.* Dorset, England: Blandford Press, 1985.

"WWII and Ford Motor Company," Michigan History, https://www.michiganhistory.leadr.msu.edu/wwii-and-ford-motor

"WW2 People's War," BBC, https://www.bbc.co.uk/history/ww2peopleswar/timeline/factfiles/nonflash/a6652055.shtml

---

Text and illustrations copyright © 2020 by Lindsay Ward
All rights reserved.

No part of this book may be reproduced, or stored in a retrieval system, or transmitted in any form or by any means, electronic, mechanical, photocopying, recording, or otherwise, without express written permission of the publisher.

Published by Two Lions, New York • www.apub.com

Amazon, the Amazon logo, and Two Lions are trademarks of Amazon.com, Inc., or its affiliates.

ISBN-13: 9781542017947 • ISBN-10: 1542017947
The illustrations were created using colored pencil and cut paper.

Back cover illustration based on historic photo of volunteers for the Women's Land Army, Cheshire, England, 1939: Historia/Shutterstock.

Book design by Abby Dening
Printed in China
First Edition
10 9 8 7 6 5 4 3 2 1